Mistletoe & Mimosas: Christmas in July: A Beach Love Story

A Non-Traditional Holiday Romance of Sunshine, Second Chances, and Unexpected Love on a Romantic Beach Getaway

Bree winterson

Copyright © 2024 by Bree winterson

All rights reserved.

No part of this book may be reproduced in any form or by any electronic or mechanical means, including information storage and retrieval systems, without written permission from the author, except for the use of brief quotations in a book review.

Contents

Prologue: Christmas in July	v
1. Arrival at Noel Beach Resort	1
2. First Impressions & Tensions	5
3. Tropical Storm Warning	10
4. The Sandman Contest	15
5. Jet Skiing Santas & Holiday Surf Lessons	21
6. The Heart of the Storm	26
7. Christmas Eve at 80 Degrees	31
8. Mistletoe & Mimosas	37
9. Love in the Keys	42
Epilogue: Christmas in July... Again?	47
Afterword from the Author: Bree Winterson	51

Prologue: Christmas in July

Phoebe swirled the half-melted ice in her glass, watching as the last cube bobbed lazily in her cranberry vodka. She barely heard the buzz of conversation in the crowded bar around her, or the music playing low in the background. It was one of those dimly lit places, cozy enough for couples but impersonal enough for people like her—people who wanted to disappear into the noise.

"He's such a jerk," Serena declared from across the table, her voice rising above the clatter of glasses. "You're better off without him. I never liked Eric anyway. Too... preppy."

Phoebe sighed. "He wasn't a jerk, not really. I mean, I didn't see it coming, but it's not like he cheated or anything. He just..." She trailed off, letting her words hang like the disappointment she'd been carrying for the last two weeks. "He just needed space."

"Space." Serena snorted, rolling her eyes. "That's guy code for 'I want to date someone else but don't want to feel guilty about it.' Classic Eric."

Phoebe forced a laugh, but it was hollow. The breakup hadn't been explosive. It had been quiet and polite, the kind that left you wondering if you'd imagined the whole relationship in the first place. Eric had been the type of guy who ironed his T-shirts and color-coded his sock drawer. Solid. Predictable. Safe. But apparently, safety wasn't enough to stop him from rekindling things with his ex-girlfriend, the one who worked at the yoga studio down the block.

Phoebe wasn't heartbroken, not exactly. She hadn't been in love with Eric—not deeply, anyway—but the rejection stung all the same. At 32, she'd thought she was past all the dating drama. They'd been together for almost a year, and she had started imagining a future, a stable life where they'd host small, tasteful Christmas dinners in their perfectly curated apartment. She hadn't expected to be sitting in a bar, picking apart her failed relationship while wondering what on earth had gone wrong.

"You know what you need?" Serena's eyes sparkled with a kind of enthusiasm that usually preceded one of her grand schemes.

"A time machine?" Phoebe asked dryly.

"No. You need a change of scenery. Some sun, some drinks, a tropical escape." Serena leaned forward, her grin widening. "You need to come with me to Florida next week."

Phoebe groaned, leaning back in her chair. "I thought that was a joke."

"Nope," Serena said, practically bouncing in her seat. "It's happening. Noel Beach Resort—Christmas in July weekend. You and me. It'll be amazing."

Phoebe stared at her friend, unsure whether to laugh or cry. "Christmas in July? You know how I feel about Christmas. And July. I'm not in the mood for fake snow and plastic Santas."

"Exactly!" Serena said, as if Phoebe's objection only made her point stronger. "That's why you need this! It's so ridiculous, you won't even have time to think about Eric. It'll be fun—cheesy fun, but still fun. Plus, it's the Florida Keys. Sunshine, cocktails, maybe a cute guy or two."

Phoebe looked down at her empty glass and thought about the alternative—spending another weekend in her apartment, watching Netflix and scrolling past Eric's Instagram stories with his new flame. Did she really want to sit through another pity party for one?

Serena gave her a knowing look, like she already knew the answer. "Look, you've been moping for two weeks. You've got to shake it off. A Christmas-themed beach resort is exactly what you need to remind yourself that life can still be fun. Even if it's ridiculous."

Phoebe took a deep breath. She hated to admit it, but Serena was probably right. She needed something, anything, to jolt her out of this fog. And who knew? Maybe the absurdity of it all would be enough to keep her distracted. Besides, how bad could a weekend of sun and sand be?

Phoebe sighed and gave a half-hearted shrug. "Fine. But if I end up spending my weekend dodging men dressed as reindeer, I'm blaming you."

Serena grinned triumphantly. "Deal. But I guarantee, by the end of the weekend, you'll be laughing. Trust me."

One week later, Phoebe found herself boarding a plane bound for the Florida Keys, her carry-on tucked under her arm and a creeping sense of dread curling in her stomach. The sun was shining, the passengers around her were cheerful, and Serena, already in full vacation mode, was scrolling through the resort's activity schedule on her phone.

Phoebe leaned her head back against the seat, staring out the window as the plane took off. She didn't want to admit it, but part of her was hoping that maybe, just maybe, this would be the distraction she needed. A few days of tropical drinks and lazy afternoons couldn't hurt, even if it was wrapped in tinsel and flashing lights.

She closed her eyes, trying to push away thoughts of Eric, of the Christmases she'd envisioned, of everything that had fallen apart. For now, all she could do was take Serena's advice and see what happened.

As the plane began its descent into the Keys, Phoebe felt a slight shift—whether it was nerves or anticipation, she wasn't sure. But she couldn't help but think that whatever awaited her at Noel Beach Resort, it would definitely be unlike any Christmas she'd ever experienced.

Arrival at Noel Beach Resort

Phoebe stepped off the shuttle bus and squinted under the intense Florida sun. The air smelled of saltwater, sunscreen, and—somehow—cinnamon? A gigantic "Welcome to Noel Beach Resort!" sign greeted them, covered in twinkling lights, glittery garland, and giant plastic candy canes that felt completely out of place against the backdrop of palm trees swaying in the humid breeze.

"Who decorates like this in July?" Phoebe muttered under her breath.

Beside her, Serena bounced with excitement. "Oh, come on, Phoebe! It's Christmas in July. Embrace the cheer!" She flung her arms wide like she was trying to hug the holiday spirit itself. "Look at this place. It's magical!"

Phoebe surveyed the scene in front of her and felt anything but enchanted. A giant inflatable snowman sat crookedly on the sand, baking in the sun, while a Santa Claus statue, complete with board shorts and sunglasses, posed next to a surfboard by the main entrance. Resort staff buzzed around in elf costumes—green felt in 80-degree heat, which seemed like a form of seasonal torture—and, yes, there were actual reindeer antlers sticking out from a nearby jet ski rental hut.

"It's a nightmare," Phoebe replied. "I could've been binge-watching true crime documentaries in my air-conditioned apartment, but no... here I am."

Serena, ever the optimist, shook her head. "You need this. After what happened with Eric, you deserve some fun. And if fun comes in the form of Christmas cheer and cocktails on the beach, so be it."

Phoebe grumbled, not wanting to be reminded of Eric, her now ex-boyfriend, who had decided two weeks ago that "he needed space." Space, of course, turned out to mean a two-year-old flame that reignited after a conveniently timed Instagram reunion. Ugh. It was enough to make her swear off relationships for good. Or at least until the end of this ridiculous holiday weekend.

As Phoebe and Serena dragged their luggage toward the lobby, an overenthusiastic bellhop appeared, dressed as an elf from head to toe, jingling with every step thanks to the tiny bells sewn into his shoes and hat.

"Merry Christmas in July!" he exclaimed with a wave, handing them each a candy cane before whisking their suitcases away.

Phoebe accepted hers reluctantly. "You've got to be kidding me," she whispered to Serena as they walked through the lobby doors, where the tropical Christmas theme only intensified. Twinkling lights were wrapped around palm trees inside the resort, fake snow clung to the railings, and a life-sized nutcracker saluted them as they passed by.

It was like stepping into a Pinterest board gone rogue.

"Phoebes, you have to admit, this is a little bit fun," Serena said, nudging her friend. "Besides, we're in the Florida Keys! Sun, sand, and—"

"An overdose of holiday spirit," Phoebe finished for her, just as a man dressed as Santa Claus whizzed by on a jet ski, waving like it was the Macy's Thanksgiving Day Parade. Serena giggled. Phoebe rolled her eyes.

They reached the check-in desk, where a cheery receptionist with a reindeer headband and a name tag that read "Rudolph" greeted them. "Welcome to Noel Beach Resort, ladies! We hope you're ready for a jolly good time. We've got our Christmas sand-sculpting contest starting this afternoon, and the sunset caroling on the beach is at six."

"Oh, I'm ready," Serena said with a grin. "Isn't this just the best, Phoebe?"

"Sure," Phoebe replied, forcing a tight smile, though internally she was already plotting how to survive the next few days.

As they turned to head toward their room, a tall figure stepped into Phoebe's path, knocking the candy cane right out of her hand. She bent down to pick it up, and when she stood, she was face-to-face with a man who looked about as thrilled to be here as she was.

"Sorry," he mumbled, clearly not sorry at all. He wore a faded T-shirt with a graphic of a shark on it, board shorts, and a permanent scowl. His sandy brown hair was tousled like he'd been dragged through the wind, and his eyes—icy blue, like the ocean just before a storm—flickered with a mix of boredom and annoyance.

"No problem," Phoebe muttered, brushing off the sand from her now broken candy cane.

"You here for the festivities, too?" the man asked dryly, his voice full of sarcasm.

"Festivities? Is that what we're calling this… extravaganza?" Phoebe gestured around them, her hand sweeping over the beach-side winter wonderland.

He smirked. "Yeah, well, it's a little over the top, but it's great if you're into kitschy holiday nonsense."

Phoebe raised an eyebrow. "And you're not?"

"Not exactly," he said. "I'm Jake, by the way. I live here...well, sort of. Work nearby. I'm only staying at the resort because of the storm coming."

"Wait—storm?" Phoebe asked, feeling a slight panic rise in her chest.

"Yeah. Tropical storm," Jake replied nonchalantly. "You know, the kind that traps you inside for the weekend. Don't worry. The resort's prepped for it. They'll probably serve piña coladas while the wind howls."

"Great," Phoebe said, deadpan. "Trapped in a Christmas nightmare with a tropical storm for a soundtrack."

Jake chuckled, but there was something oddly comforting in his easy, no-nonsense demeanor. "You'll survive. Just steer clear of the elves on jet skis."

Phoebe cracked a tiny smile, but before she could respond, Serena rushed over, beaming from ear to ear. "Our room has a balcony overlooking the beach! Come on, Phoebes, let's get settled in!" She grabbed Phoebe's hand, pulling her away from Jake.

As they headed toward the elevator, Phoebe glanced back, catching one last look at Jake. He stood there, watching the madness unfold around him with the same dry amusement she felt.

Maybe, just maybe, this weekend wouldn't be as unbearable as she'd thought.

First Impressions & Tensions

Phoebe sank into a lounge chair by the resort's lagoon-style pool, sunglasses perched on her nose, and a mimosa clutched in her hand. She had hoped the tropical setting would help ease her tension, but even here, surrounded by sun and palm trees, it was impossible to escape the relentless Christmas in July theme.

Cheerful jingles played from hidden speakers, drowning out the sound of ocean waves, while resort staff—still decked out in elf attire—zipped back and forth, handing out peppermint-scented towels and trays of eggnog. A woman in a Mrs. Claus swimsuit led a group of children in a game of "Pin the Nose on Rudolph" near the shallow end of the pool.

Phoebe sighed heavily, taking a long sip of her mimosa. "This is not what I had in mind when I agreed to this trip," she muttered.

Just then, a shadow fell across her lounge chair. She glanced up and spotted Jake standing a few feet away, wearing the same faded shark T-shirt and board shorts from earlier. He held a cup of coffee in one hand and looked just as unimpressed as she felt.

"Let me guess," Jake said, his voice dripping with sarcasm, "you're enjoying the magical ambiance?"

Phoebe rolled her eyes. "Oh, it's everything I ever dreamed of and more. Nothing says 'relaxing vacation' like nonstop Christmas carols and elves on rollerblades."

Jake chuckled, taking a seat on the lounge chair next to her. "Yeah, it's a lot. But hey, at least they've got mimosas."

Phoebe raised her glass slightly in agreement. "Small mercies."

For a moment, they sat in silence, both of them watching as a team of resort staff set up a Christmas tree near the pool, decorating it with seashell ornaments and tinsel that fluttered in the breeze.

"So," Phoebe began, breaking the silence, "you mentioned something about being stuck here because of a storm?"

Jake nodded, taking a sip of his coffee. "Yeah. I'm a marine biologist. I work at a research facility not far from here, but with the tropical storm coming in, they had to shut down our fieldwork for the weekend. Figured I might as well ride it out here since the resort is more equipped for it than my place."

"A marine biologist?" Phoebe said, raising an eyebrow. "So you study fish and stuff?"

Jake smirked. "Something like that. Sharks, mostly."

"Sharks?" Phoebe glanced at his shirt, noticing the faded image of a great white on the front. "Okay, that's actually kind of cool."

Jake shrugged like it was no big deal, but there was a hint of pride in his eyes. "It's not bad. I've been working on this big project tracking shark migration patterns in the Keys. Fascinating stuff, but most people aren't as excited about it as I am."

Phoebe took another sip of her drink. "Well, it definitely beats what I do. I'm an editor at a publishing house in New York. So, unless you're really into debating comma placement or arguing over cover designs, my job probably wouldn't sound all that thrilling to you."

"Depends," Jake said, leaning back in his chair. "Are you one of those grammar sticklers who corrects people's texts?"

Phoebe laughed. "Only sometimes. But it's mostly just long hours and trying to keep authors on deadline."

"Sounds rough," Jake replied, though his tone was playful. "I think I'd take my chances with the sharks."

Phoebe smirked. "At least sharks don't send passive-aggressive emails."

Jake raised his coffee cup in a mock toast. "Touché."

For a few seconds, it seemed like they were actually getting along. But then, as if on cue, a particularly loud burst of Christmas music blared from the speakers, breaking the moment. Phoebe grimaced, her mood souring again.

"Seriously, who thought this was a good idea?" she muttered, gesturing to the surrounding Christmas chaos. "It's the middle of July. Who needs this much holiday cheer?"

"Not me," Jake said with a shrug. "But then again, I'm not exactly the festive type."

"Clearly," Phoebe shot back, eyeing his grungy T-shirt. "I mean, I'm no Christmas fanatic, but this whole 'Bah Humbug' thing you've got going on is a little much."

Jake raised an eyebrow. "Oh, I'm the one with the problem? You're the one who looks like she'd rather be anywhere else but here."

"Maybe I would," Phoebe snapped, her irritation rising. "This wasn't my idea, okay? I got dragged here by my friend who thought a Christmas-themed beach resort was the perfect way to 'get over' my breakup."

"Ah," Jake said, a knowing look crossing his face. "The breakup trip. That explains a lot."

"What's that supposed to mean?" Phoebe asked, narrowing her eyes.

Jake shrugged. "Just that I've seen it before. People come to these resorts to escape their problems, but all they do is complain about everything. Maybe it's not the resort that's the problem."

Phoebe's jaw tightened. "Look, just because I'm not swooning over fake snow and candy canes doesn't mean I'm wallowing in self-pity."

Jake held up his hands in mock surrender. "Hey, I'm just saying, maybe lighten up a little. It's not the end of the world."

"Lighten up?" Phoebe scoffed. "This from the guy who looks like he'd rather swim with sharks than spend five minutes at a Christmas party."

Jake's smirk returned. "Fair enough. But at least I'm not letting it ruin my weekend."

Phoebe opened her mouth to retort but found herself at a loss for words. He wasn't entirely wrong. She had spent the entire morning mentally picking apart every little thing that bothered her, instead of just—what was it Serena had said?—embracing the cheer.

"I just don't get it," Phoebe said after a pause. "The forced festiveness, the tacky decorations—it feels so fake."

Jake leaned back in his chair, crossing his arms. "Maybe. Or maybe some people just like a little extra joy, even if it comes in the form of plastic reindeer and palm trees wrapped in Christmas lights."

Phoebe glanced over at a group of kids laughing as they decorated sandcastles with miniature wreaths and ornaments. Serena was right there with them, her face lit up with the kind of joy Phoebe hadn't felt in a long time.

Maybe Jake had a point.

"I'll think about it," Phoebe finally said, offering a reluctant smile.

Jake nodded, his expression softening just a fraction. "Good. In the meantime, if you need a break from the holiday overload, you know where to find me. I'll be the guy not wearing antlers."

Phoebe laughed despite herself. "Noted."

As Jake got up to leave, Phoebe couldn't help but feel that, for all their differences—and the tension that came with it—there was something refreshing about his bluntness. Maybe the weekend wouldn't be as unbearable as she'd thought. Maybe it would even surprise her.

But she wasn't about to admit that just yet.

Tropical Storm Warning

Phoebe stared out the large bay windows of the resort's lobby, watching the palm trees sway wildly in the growing wind. Dark clouds rolled in, blotting out the sun, and the waves crashed aggressively against the shore, sending mist into the air. The once vibrant beach now looked more ominous than inviting.

A voice crackled over the resort's intercom, cheerful yet annoyingly persistent: "Attention guests! Due to the approaching tropical storm, we advise everyone to remain indoors. But don't worry! Our 'Tropical Christmas Eve' party will still be held in the main ballroom tonight, complete with holiday cocktails, a buffet, and plenty of Christmas cheer to go around!"

Phoebe groaned audibly, her patience running thin. "Of course," she muttered. "Because what better way to distract people from a potential natural disaster than with more tinsel and eggnog?"

She heard Serena squeal from the lobby gift shop, where she was inspecting a snowflake bikini with glittering rhinestones. "Isn't this the cutest thing? I'm totally wearing it to the party tonight!"

Serena's eyes sparkled with excitement, completely unfazed by the impending storm outside.

"I think I'll pass," Phoebe replied flatly, her arms crossed over her chest. The idea of mingling with resort guests in Santa hats while the wind howled outside was the last thing she wanted to do.

"You can't hide in the bungalow all night," Serena said, pulling Phoebe away from the window and into the store. "It'll be fun! Come on, just give it a chance. Besides, I heard they're having a gingerbread house contest—how can you say no to that?"

Phoebe shot her friend a look. "Very easily."

Serena sighed, grabbing a novelty elf hat off the shelf and plopping it onto Phoebe's head. "You need to loosen up. It's not like we can leave, anyway. Might as well make the best of it!"

Phoebe pulled off the hat, shaking her head. "I think I'll make the best of it by staying as far away from Christmas karaoke as possible."

Serena pouted, but Phoebe was already making up her mind. She would retreat to the bungalow, curl up with a book, and wait for this whole ridiculous weekend to blow over—literally and figuratively.

LATER THAT AFTERNOON, after successfully avoiding the ever-increasing festivity, Phoebe made her way back to her beach bungalow. She could hear the wind picking up, rattling the shutters as she walked, and the occasional gust blew her hair into her face. The storm was clearly getting closer.

As she reached the door to her bungalow, she heard a familiar voice behind her.

"Escaping the party, huh?"

Phoebe turned to find Jake standing on the porch of the bungalow next to hers, holding a laptop under one arm and a bottle of wine in the other. His tousled hair was even messier than before, thanks to the wind, but he still wore the same nonchalant expression that seemed permanently etched on his face.

"Let me guess," Phoebe replied, "you're not in the mood for Christmas limbo, either?"

Jake smirked. "Not exactly my thing. Plus, I've got work to do." He lifted the laptop slightly as if to emphasize his point, but his eyes drifted to the wine bottle. "Though I was thinking of taking a break."

Phoebe eyed the wine. "Taking a break, huh? And here I thought you were all work and no play."

"I can multitask," Jake said with a grin. He nodded toward her door. "You, uh, want to join? I could use the company—purely for scientific purposes, of course."

Phoebe hesitated, still torn between her desire to be alone and her curiosity about the man who had been just as frustrated by the resort's holiday mania. She wasn't exactly in the mood to bond, but then again, her other option was sitting in her bungalow with nothing but the howling wind and her own grumpiness.

With a sigh, she gave in. "Fine. But if you start talking about sharks, I'm out."

Jake chuckled. "Deal."

They moved inside Phoebe's bungalow, where she immediately noticed how much cozier it felt compared to the chaos outside. The dim lighting and soft hum of the air conditioner provided a peaceful contrast to the frenzy happening elsewhere in the resort. Jake uncorked the bottle of wine, and Phoebe grabbed two glasses from the kitchenette.

"Chardonnay," Jake said, handing her a glass. "Not exactly holiday punch, but I figured it would do."

Phoebe raised her glass in a mock toast. "To avoiding Christmas-themed disasters."

"And tropical storms," Jake added with a smirk. They clinked their glasses and both took a sip.

For a while, they sat in comfortable silence, the only sound the wind pushing against the bungalow's windows. Phoebe was grateful for the reprieve from the holiday madness, and though she didn't know Jake well, there was something oddly calming about being around him. Maybe it was the fact that he wasn't pushing her to "have fun" or "embrace the cheer," like everyone else seemed to be doing.

"Tell me," Phoebe said after a moment, breaking the silence, "how did you end up stuck here with all this Christmas craziness? I mean, you don't seem like the type to voluntarily book a stay at a holiday resort."

Jake chuckled, swirling the wine in his glass. "I didn't. Like I said, I'm just here because of the storm. My team's research was supposed to wrap up tomorrow, but with the weather, we had to call it early. The resort was the closest place that still had rooms available."

Phoebe raised an eyebrow. "Research?"

"Shark migration," Jake replied. "I'm tracking their movements through the Keys, trying to understand how environmental changes are affecting their patterns. It's...important work."

Phoebe leaned back on the couch, intrigued despite herself. "Okay, I'll admit, that actually sounds interesting. But I still don't get why you'd stay at a place like this. A marine biologist at a Christmas resort—it's like a bad punchline."

Jake smirked. "Trust me, I didn't exactly plan it this way. But here I am, stuck in Christmas hell with the rest of you."

Phoebe laughed, feeling some of her earlier frustration begin to melt away. "You and me both."

They continued to sip their wine, the conversation flowing more easily now. For all their differences, there was a strange comfort in sharing their mutual disdain for the resort's forced holiday spirit. As the storm continued to build outside, it felt like they were in their own little bubble, insulated from the chaos.

After a while, Phoebe leaned back, her head resting against the couch. "You know, this is actually kind of nice."

Jake raised an eyebrow. "The storm?"

"No," Phoebe said with a smile, "this. Sitting here, drinking wine, not having to pretend I'm having the time of my life with people I don't know."

Jake smiled, the first genuine smile she'd seen from him all weekend. "Yeah. It's not so bad."

Phoebe looked over at him, feeling the tension between them shift into something less antagonistic. Maybe it was the wine, or maybe it was just the relief of finding someone who felt as out of place as she did. Either way, for the first time since arriving at Noel Beach Resort, she didn't feel completely miserable.

And that, she thought with a small smile, was something to hold on to.

The Sandman Contest

The morning after the storm dawned bright and clear, the sky scrubbed clean of clouds and the air warm but no longer heavy with humidity. Phoebe stood on the bungalow's small porch, sipping coffee and watching the waves roll gently onto the shore, relieved that the tropical storm had passed with minimal damage. Despite the wild winds and occasional thunder, the resort had survived mostly unscathed, and it seemed the staff was eager to get back to their regularly scheduled festivities.

"I hope that storm knocked some sense into everyone," Phoebe muttered under her breath, though she knew better.

As if on cue, Serena burst through the door, a flurry of excitement and energy as usual. "Phoebes! You're not going to believe it—they're still doing the sandman-building contest today!" she announced, practically bouncing on her heels. "We have to sign up! It'll be so fun!"

"Fun? You mean standing in the sun, surrounded by people competing to make the most elaborate Christmas monstrosity out of sand?" Phoebe arched an eyebrow.

Serena didn't miss a beat. "Exactly! Come on, it'll be a blast! Besides, you've been moping around enough. It's time to get into the holiday spirit."

Phoebe groaned but knew there was no point in resisting. Serena had made it her personal mission to drag her out of her post-breakup funk, and a sandman contest was just the kind of ridiculousness she lived for.

"Fine," Phoebe said, setting down her coffee. "But don't expect me to sculpt anything more advanced than a lopsided snowball."

Serena squealed, grabbing Phoebe's hand and pulling her toward the beach. "This is going to be amazing!"

By the time they reached the contest area, the beach was buzzing with activity. A large banner that read **"Noel Beach Resort Sandman Building Contest!"** flapped in the breeze, and dozens of guests were already setting up their tools, ready to transform piles of sand into Christmas masterpieces. Some of the more enthusiastic participants had even brought props—mini Santa hats, tinsel, and plastic carrot noses.

Phoebe scanned the crowd and wasn't surprised to spot Jake standing off to the side, looking about as thrilled as she felt. He was talking to a man wearing a brightly colored Hawaiian shirt and cargo shorts, who was gesturing wildly with a clipboard in hand. The man's animated expression contrasted sharply with Jake's usual laid-back demeanor.

"Who's that?" Phoebe asked, nodding in their direction as Serena tied back her hair, prepping for sand-building battle.

"That's Jake's boss, Dr. Carmichael," Serena explained, her eyes widening as she watched the man wave his arms around. "He runs the marine biology center nearby. Apparently, he's super into these resort activities."

Phoebe chuckled. "Poor Jake. He's probably being forced into this."

As if he'd heard his name, Jake glanced over at them, locking eyes with Phoebe. He gave her a resigned shrug, as if to say, *Yep, I'm stuck doing this, too.*

Before Phoebe could feel any pity for him, Serena handed her a small shovel. "Let's go grab a spot! We need prime sand real estate."

They found a relatively empty area near the water, where the sand was soft and damp, perfect for sculpting. Phoebe knelt down and half-heartedly started to pile sand into a rough mound. Meanwhile, Serena was already sketching out grand plans for their sandman, babbling about adding a mermaid tail or maybe even reindeer antlers made out of driftwood.

"Oh, this is going to be epic," Serena said, eyes gleaming with determination. "Just you wait."

Before Phoebe could roll her eyes in response, a voice interrupted.

"Looks like we're in this together after all," Jake said, stepping up behind her, his voice laced with dry amusement. He dropped a bucket next to her mound of sand, his arms crossed as if bracing for the absurdity ahead.

Phoebe looked up, confused. "What do you mean?"

"My boss," Jake explained, gesturing toward Dr. Carmichael, who was already chatting enthusiastically with other contestants. "He thought it would be 'good for team morale' if I partnered up with another guest for the contest."

Phoebe groaned inwardly, though part of her wasn't entirely surprised. "Let me guess—I'm the lucky partner?"

"Looks that way," Jake said, his smirk widening. "Hope you've got some serious sandcastle skills."

"Skills? I'm here against my will," Phoebe replied, tossing a handful of sand at his feet.

Jake chuckled. "Guess we're both in the same boat, then."

For a while, they worked in silence, each of them sculpting their own portion of the sandman—Phoebe focusing on the base, while Jake shaped the body. Their usual bickering subsided as they became absorbed in the task, the rhythm of piling and smoothing the sand surprisingly soothing. The sun beat down, but there was a pleasant breeze coming off the ocean, and Phoebe found herself relaxing, despite the absurdity of the situation.

"You know," Jake said, pausing to inspect their work, "this thing is actually starting to look decent."

Phoebe glanced over at the sandman, which now had a somewhat recognizable shape—two rounded sand globes stacked on top of each other, with a seashell smile and driftwood arms. "Not bad for two people who would rather be anywhere else," she admitted, brushing some stray sand off her knees.

Jake crouched down beside her, close enough that Phoebe could smell the salt from the ocean still clinging to his skin. "You're not going to add some over-the-top accessories like everyone else?" he teased, nodding toward a nearby group who were adorning their sandman with starfish and Christmas ornaments.

Phoebe snorted. "No thanks. I think we're going for the minimalist look."

"Good choice," Jake said, his voice taking on a teasing lilt. "Though I don't know, a Santa hat might really bring out the personality in this guy."

Phoebe rolled her eyes but couldn't help smiling. "Please. You're just as bad as the rest of them."

Jake's expression softened, his usual sarcasm fading for a moment. "Maybe. Or maybe I just think you're taking this whole 'holiday hater' thing too seriously."

Phoebe looked up at him, surprised by the gentle tone in his voice. "Is that your professional opinion, Dr. Shark?"

Jake grinned. "Hey, I'm just saying—it's not all bad. Sometimes it's okay to enjoy the ridiculous stuff."

Phoebe raised an eyebrow. "You sure about that? You've been pretty grumpy about this whole Christmas in July thing."

Jake shrugged. "Maybe I've had a change of heart. Or maybe I'm just realizing it's not so bad if you've got the right company."

The playful banter between them shifted, the tension that had simmered since they'd met now giving way to something warmer, something that felt a lot like...flirtation. Phoebe could feel the blush rising in her cheeks, but she quickly turned her attention back to the sandman.

"You know, I never would've guessed," Phoebe said, smoothing the sand with her hands, "but for a guy who studies sharks, you're pretty good at building snowmen."

Jake chuckled. "I'm a man of many talents."

Phoebe smirked, shaking her head. "Oh yeah? Like what?"

Jake leaned in, close enough that she could see the spark of amusement in his ocean-blue eyes. "Guess you'll just have to stick around to find out."

For a moment, they simply stared at each other, the playful bickering forgotten as the breeze carried the sound of distant laughter and crashing waves. Phoebe felt her heart skip a beat, realizing that maybe—just maybe—this unexpected holiday weekend wasn't turning out as miserable as she'd feared.

But before she could respond, Serena bounded over, her eyes wide with excitement. "Oh my God, you guys! Our sandman is the best one here. We might actually win!"

Jake and Phoebe both laughed, the tension between them dissolving into shared amusement. Whatever strange shift had happened between them, they weren't quite ready to acknowledge it just yet.

"Let's not get ahead of ourselves," Phoebe said with a grin, glancing at their sand creation.

But as Jake smiled back at her, something told Phoebe that they'd already won something far more interesting than a silly contest.

Jet Skiing Santas & Holiday Surf Lessons

The beach was a riot of color and movement as Phoebe and Jake walked down toward the shore, both wearing the same mix of reluctance and amusement that had carried them through most of the weekend. Brightly colored surfboards lined the sand, and a group of resort staff dressed in Santa costumes zipped around on jet skis, causing waves of laughter and cheers from the guests. The absurdity of the scene wasn't lost on Phoebe, and she shook her head as one of the Santas blew an enthusiastic ho-ho-ho into the air, his red suit flapping comically in the breeze.

"I still can't believe we're doing this," Phoebe muttered, adjusting the strap on her wetsuit. "Holiday-themed surf lessons? Who even thinks of this stuff?"

"Someone with a twisted sense of humor," Jake replied with a smirk, pulling on a rash guard. "But hey, if we're going to be stuck here, might as well embrace the ridiculousness."

Phoebe glanced over at him, trying to suppress the grin tugging at the corners of her mouth. The sun caught the golden highlights in his sandy brown hair, which was messier than usual from the wind, and his usual sarcastic edge seemed to soften in the playful atmosphere. For the first time, she could see Jake relaxing into the moment, and something about that made her feel lighter, too.

"All right, everyone!" shouted a surf instructor dressed as an elf, his pointy hat flopping around as he clapped his hands for attention. "Gather around! It's time for your holiday surf lesson! We've got some Santas on standby for extra help, so don't be shy—let's catch some festive waves!"

Phoebe snorted. "Festive waves? Really?"

Jake chuckled beside her, leaning in a little closer. "I'm starting to think these guys have too much time on their hands."

They joined the group as the instructor led them through a quick tutorial on the basics of surfing—paddling out, popping up on the board, and maintaining balance. Phoebe tried to focus on the instructions, but the constant interruptions from jet-ski-riding Santas made it hard to take anything seriously. One particularly exuberant Santa nearly collided with a group of beginners, sending up a spray of water and good-natured laughter.

"Remind me again why we're doing this?" Phoebe asked, eyeing the chaotic scene.

Jake smirked. "Because deep down, you love the chaos. You just won't admit it."

Phoebe shot him a look. "Oh, please. You're just as cynical as I am."

"True," Jake admitted. "But at least I can laugh at it."

With the lesson over, they headed out into the water, each of them dragging a surfboard behind them. The waves weren't particularly large—thankfully, considering Phoebe's lack of surfing experience—but they were steady enough to give her a decent challenge. She paddled out, feeling the cool saltwater splash against her face, and tried to ignore the sound of more jet-skiing Santas zooming by.

After a few failed attempts at standing up on the board,

Phoebe finally managed to catch a wave, wobbling unsteadily but staying upright long enough to feel a rush of exhilaration. She heard Jake cheering from a few feet away, and for a moment, her frustration melted into genuine joy.

"You did it!" Jake called out, a rare smile lighting up his face.

Phoebe beamed, paddling back toward him. "I actually did it! I didn't think I would."

"See? You're more capable than you give yourself credit for," Jake said, his tone playful but with a hint of sincerity. He caught a wave effortlessly, standing on the board with an ease that made Phoebe slightly envious. As he glided past her, he gave a little salute, causing her to roll her eyes.

"Show-off," she muttered, though she couldn't stop smiling.

The rest of the lesson passed in a blur of laughter, falls, and playful competition as Phoebe and Jake challenged each other to stay on their boards longer or catch the biggest waves. The festive atmosphere, once an annoyance, started to feel contagious, and Phoebe found herself laughing more freely, letting go of the tension she'd been carrying since she arrived at the resort.

After an hour of surfing, they finally retreated to the shore, exhausted but grinning.

"You're not half bad," Jake said as they flopped onto the sand, their surfboards abandoned nearby.

Phoebe stretched out on her towel, catching her breath. "I'm going to pretend that was a compliment."

Jake chuckled, glancing out at the ocean where more guests were still attempting to ride the waves. His expression softened, and for the first time, he looked less guarded, more open. Phoebe sensed a shift in him, as if the energy of the beach and the silliness of the day had worn down his usual defenses.

After a moment, Jake sighed and leaned back on his elbows, the sun casting a warm glow on his face. "You know, I used to love the holidays. When I was a kid, it was my favorite time of year."

Phoebe looked over at him, surprised by the sudden personal confession. "Really? You? Mr. 'I Hate Christmas in July'?"

Jake nodded, his gaze distant. "Yeah. My mom made a big deal out of it every year—decorating the house, baking cookies, the whole thing. She was really into it."

Phoebe stayed quiet, sensing there was more to the story.

"But after she died, my dad…well, he kind of checked out," Jake continued, his voice quieter now. "He didn't want to do any of it anymore. No tree, no decorations, nothing. It was like he thought pretending the holidays didn't exist would make it easier."

Phoebe felt a pang of sympathy. "That must have been tough."

Jake shrugged, though his expression was tight. "I guess I just stopped caring about it after that. It felt pointless, like the whole thing was just a reminder of what wasn't there anymore."

Phoebe nodded, understanding more than she expected. "I get that. The holidays can be hard when you're not in the mood for all the cheer."

"Exactly," Jake said, glancing over at her. "So when I see all this—" He gestured toward the beach, where a Santa was now attempting to surf while still wearing his full suit. "—I can't help but feel like it's all a little…much."

Phoebe laughed softly. "Yeah, I get that too. But maybe—just maybe—it doesn't always have to be a bad thing."

Jake raised an eyebrow, his smirk returning. "Is that you, embracing the holiday spirit?"

Phoebe shrugged, a smile tugging at her lips. "I'm just saying, maybe it's not all terrible. Sometimes, ridiculousness can be…fun."

Jake studied her for a moment, the vulnerability still there but mixed with something lighter now. "Maybe you're right."

For a while, they sat in companionable silence, watching the waves roll in and out. Phoebe felt the sun warming her skin, the laughter from the beachgoers in the distance, and Jake's quiet presence beside her. It was peaceful, almost perfect, and for the first time in a long while, Phoebe realized she wasn't thinking about Eric, or her breakup, or anything else that had weighed her down before this trip.

Maybe, she thought, this Christmas in July thing wasn't so bad after all.

And maybe, just maybe, there was more to Jake than she'd originally thought—more than just the gruff exterior and sarcastic humor. Beneath it all, there was someone who had been hurt, someone who had learned to protect himself with cynicism and wit. But today, for the first time, she saw glimpses of something softer, something real.

As the sun began to dip lower in the sky, Phoebe glanced over at Jake, a playful glint in her eyes. "So, what's next? Jet-skiing with Santa, or are we calling it a day?"

Jake grinned, his blue eyes sparkling. "I think we've earned a break. But I wouldn't rule out jet-skiing just yet."

Phoebe laughed, feeling lighter than she had in months. Maybe she wasn't quite ready to dive headfirst into the holiday madness, but with Jake beside her, the idea didn't seem quite so terrible anymore.

The Heart of the Storm

The resort's Christmas karaoke night was in full swing, and the atmosphere in the open-air lounge was buzzing with a mix of festive cheer and bad renditions of holiday classics. Phoebe sat at the bar, nursing a gingerbread martini that Serena had insisted she try. The flashing lights on the stage reflected off the palm trees outside, and the whole scene felt like something out of a bizarre dream—Christmas lights, beachwear, and the occasional off-key version of *"Jingle Bell Rock."*

"Are you sure you don't want to sing something?" Serena asked, bouncing on her stool as she watched a group of women in elf hats butcher *"All I Want for Christmas Is You."*

"I'm positive," Phoebe replied, trying not to wince at the high-pitched notes. "I'm still recovering from surfing Santas."

Serena laughed, but there was a gleam in her eye that Phoebe knew all too well—the gleam of a woman who wasn't going to let her off the hook so easily. "Oh, come on. I bet you and Jake could do a duet. You've been spending enough time together to have your own theme song by now."

Phoebe shot her a look. "Very funny."

Serena smirked, clearly not ready to drop the subject. "Seriously though, Phoebes, what's going on with you two? You guys have been glued to each other for the last two days."

Phoebe took a long sip of her drink, trying to brush off the question. "We're just...having fun. It's nothing serious."

"Really?" Serena leaned in, lowering her voice. "Because from where I'm sitting, it looks like there's a little more going on than just 'fun.'"

Phoebe hesitated, glancing toward the far corner of the room where Jake was standing, talking to his boss, Dr. Carmichael, who was still dressed in his usual Hawaiian shirt despite the Christmas theme. Jake looked relaxed, his arms crossed as he listened to whatever his boss was saying, but Phoebe noticed that he glanced over at her every now and then, like he was checking to make sure she was still there.

"I don't know," Phoebe finally said, her voice softer now. "He's...different. I like him, but I don't know if I'm ready for anything serious. After Eric, I just feel—" She paused, searching for the right word. "Cautious, I guess. And Jake, he's so closed off. I don't know what he really wants."

Serena frowned, her playful demeanor fading. "You think it's just a fling?"

"I don't know," Phoebe admitted, swirling her drink absentmindedly. "It's been great, but it's hard to tell if this is just...a holiday thing. You know? We're in this weird bubble here, with all the Christmas craziness. I don't even know what our dynamic would be like outside of this."

Unbeknownst to Phoebe, Jake had walked toward the bar at that exact moment, heading over to grab another drink before joining the group. But as he approached, he overheard the tail end of Phoebe's conversation with Serena—the part where she voiced her uncertainty about their connection.

His expression hardened as her words hit him, each one

sinking deeper than Phoebe intended. *Just a holiday thing?* That simple phrase echoed in his mind, stirring up a mess of emotions he wasn't prepared to deal with.

Without saying a word, Jake turned on his heel and walked back toward the other side of the lounge, a heavy weight settling in his chest. He knew he shouldn't have expected anything more—he'd been careful not to get too close, not to let his guard down. But still, hearing Phoebe's doubts made it feel all too real.

As the night wore on, Phoebe noticed that Jake had been unusually quiet. He had rejoined the group but seemed distant, his easy smile replaced with something more guarded. It was as if he had retreated into himself, pulling away from her with a cool detachment she hadn't seen before.

Serena, sensing the tension, disappeared to join a group of people singing a particularly terrible version of *"Frosty the Snowman,"* leaving Phoebe and Jake alone at the table. Phoebe shifted in her seat, trying to shake off the awkwardness that had settled between them.

"Everything okay?" she asked, her voice hesitant.

Jake gave her a tight smile. "Yeah. Just tired. It's been a long day."

Phoebe frowned. She could tell something was bothering him, but she didn't know what. "You sure? You seem…off."

Jake shrugged, his tone casual but distant. "I'm fine. Maybe I just need to get back to work. All this Christmas stuff is starting to get to me."

Phoebe's stomach twisted. There was something in his voice, something cold and final, that made her heart drop. She searched his face for any sign of the warmth and connection they'd shared earlier in the day, but it was gone, replaced by a mask of indifference.

"Is this about earlier?" she asked, the words tumbling out before she could stop herself. "Did I do something?"

Jake shook his head, not meeting her eyes. "No. It's not you. I just…I need to get back to my project. This whole trip has been a distraction."

"A distraction?" Phoebe repeated, her voice sharp with hurt. "That's all this has been to you?"

Jake ran a hand through his hair, looking frustrated. "That's not what I meant."

"Then what did you mean?" Phoebe pressed, her heart pounding in her chest. "Because right now, it feels like you're pulling away."

Jake's jaw tightened, and for a moment, he didn't say anything. When he finally spoke, his voice was low and filled with tension. "Maybe we're both pulling away. I heard what you said to Serena."

Phoebe's eyes widened in shock. "You…you heard that?"

Jake nodded, his expression unreadable. "Yeah. You're not ready for anything serious. You think this is just a holiday fling."

Phoebe's throat tightened. "That's not—I didn't mean it like that. I was just…I don't know, trying to figure things out. I'm confused, Jake."

"So am I," Jake admitted, his voice softer now but no less strained. "Look, I get it. You've been through a lot, and I'm not exactly the most open guy in the world. But hearing you say that made me realize maybe I'm not what you need right now."

Phoebe felt her heart sink. This wasn't how she'd wanted things to go. She hadn't meant to hurt him, hadn't meant to push him away, but somehow, that's exactly what was happening.

"Jake," she began, her voice barely above a whisper, "I didn't mean to make it sound like this doesn't matter to me. I just…I don't know what this is."

Jake nodded, his expression pained. "I get it. But maybe we're just not on the same page."

With that, Jake stood up, his chair scraping against the floor as he pushed it back. Phoebe watched helplessly as he grabbed his jacket and headed toward the exit, his retreat feeling like a sudden, unexpected storm she hadn't seen coming.

As he disappeared into the night, leaving the festive chaos of the karaoke bar behind, Phoebe sat frozen, her mind racing.

Had this whole connection been a fleeting moment, something destined to fizzle out once the holiday decorations came down? Or had she let her own fears and uncertainty drive away the one person who had made her feel something real again?

Serena returned to the table, her laughter fading as she took in Phoebe's stricken expression. "What happened?" she asked, sitting down beside her.

Phoebe shook her head, her heart heavy with confusion and regret. "I think I just ruined everything."

Serena reached for her hand, offering a comforting squeeze. "No, you didn't. If Jake's pulling away, it's not just on you."

Phoebe wanted to believe that, but deep down, she couldn't shake the feeling that maybe Jake was right—that they weren't on the same page, and that whatever they had was slipping through her fingers before she could even figure out what it was.

And as the night wore on, with the sound of Christmas karaoke echoing in the background, Phoebe was left with the sinking realization that this holiday storm wasn't just about the weather—it was about the heart.

Christmas Eve at 80 Degrees

The beach was alive with the glow of tiki torches and string lights, their warm, flickering light casting a magical ambiance over the resort's grand "Christmas Eve" dinner. Tables were set up on the sand, decorated with seashells and holly, blending the tropical with the traditional in a way that was as strange as it was charming. A bonfire crackled at the center of the gathering, sending sparks into the humid night air, while the resort staff—still clad in holiday-themed attire—served trays of seafood, cocktails, and tropical desserts.

Phoebe stood on the edge of the festivities, holding a glass of sangria and trying to shake off the knot of tension that had settled in her stomach since her confrontation with Jake the night before. She'd avoided him all day, and from what she could tell, he'd been doing the same. It was easier that way, even if it left her with a nagging sense of unfinished business.

The resort's version of a Christmas Eve celebration was both ridiculous and beautiful in its own way—lobster tail and coconut shrimp replacing turkey and stuffing, the ocean breeze warm instead of a winter chill. But despite the festive atmosphere, Phoebe felt out of place, as if she were standing on the outside of something she didn't quite understand.

"Stop brooding," Serena's voice chimed from behind her, pulling her from her thoughts. Phoebe turned to see her friend, glowing in a red sundress, holding a drink with a little reindeer stirrer in it. "It's Christmas Eve! You should be having fun, not standing over here by yourself looking all melancholy."

Phoebe sighed. "I'm not brooding. I'm just...thinking."

"Thinking about Jake?" Serena asked with a knowing smile.

Phoebe shot her a look. "Maybe."

Serena glanced across the beach, where Jake stood near the bonfire, talking with his boss, Dr. Carmichael, who was animatedly telling some story. Jake, however, looked distracted, his eyes scanning the crowd every now and then as if searching for something—or someone. Phoebe tried to ignore the way her pulse quickened when his gaze briefly landed on her before shifting away again.

"He hasn't taken his eyes off you all night," Serena pointed out, nudging Phoebe's shoulder.

"That's not true," Phoebe muttered, even though she had noticed it too. "We...I don't even know what we are right now. I think I messed it up."

Serena shook her head. "If you two have something real, you didn't mess it up. You just need to talk to him. Clear the air."

Phoebe sighed, taking a sip of her drink. "He doesn't want to talk. He made that pretty clear last night."

"Maybe he's waiting for you to make the first move," Serena suggested. "It's obvious there's something between you. Don't let your fear get in the way."

Before Phoebe could respond, Serena gave her a gentle push toward the bonfire. "Go. Now."

Phoebe hesitated, feeling a rush of nerves, but Serena's words echoed in her head. *Don't let your fear get in the way.* With a deep breath, she turned toward the fire, where Jake was still standing.

ON THE OTHER side of the bonfire, Jake stood with Dr. Carmichael, barely listening as his boss regaled him with yet another story about his marine adventures. His mind was elsewhere—on Phoebe. Every time he glanced her way, the same mix of frustration and longing churned in his chest. He hated that he'd pulled away from her the night before, but hearing her talk about their connection as "just a holiday thing" had stirred up old fears he thought he'd buried. It felt too close to his past, too familiar to the hurt he'd spent years trying to outrun.

"So, what's going on with you and that girl over there?" Dr. Carmichael's voice broke through his thoughts, and Jake blinked, realizing his boss was now giving him a pointed look.

Jake frowned. "What? Nothing's going on."

Dr. Carmichael raised an eyebrow, unconvinced. "Come on, Jake. I've been around long enough to know when something's brewing between two people. You've been watching her all night."

Jake shifted uncomfortably. "It's complicated."

"Doesn't have to be," his boss replied, taking a sip of his rum punch. "I don't know what happened, but whatever it is, don't let it slip away because you're too stubborn or scared to talk about it."

Jake let out a long breath, his gaze drifting back to Phoebe, who was now making her way toward the bonfire, her eyes flickering with the same uncertainty he felt. His heart twisted. Maybe his boss was right. Maybe it didn't have to be complicated—if he was willing to face his own fears.

. . .

Phoebe approached the bonfire, her heart pounding in her chest as she stepped closer to Jake. He looked up as she neared, his expression guarded but softened by something that looked a lot like regret.

"Hey," she said, her voice quiet as she stopped a few feet away.

"Hey," Jake replied, his eyes meeting hers. There was a long pause, the tension between them thick and unresolved, but neither of them moved.

Phoebe swallowed, gathering her courage. "Can we talk?"

Jake nodded, gesturing to a spot away from the crowd, closer to the water where the sound of the waves would drown out the chatter of the party. They walked in silence, the warm sand soft beneath their feet, the tiki torches casting long shadows as they left the bonfire behind.

When they reached the edge of the beach, Jake turned to face her, his hands shoved in his pockets. "Look, about last night—"

"No, let me go first," Phoebe interrupted, taking a deep breath. "I didn't mean for things to get so messed up. What you overheard...that wasn't the whole picture. I wasn't saying that this—" She gestured between them. "—doesn't matter to me. I just...I'm scared."

Jake's expression softened, the tension in his shoulders easing as he listened. "Scared of what?"

Phoebe looked out at the ocean, her voice low but steady. "Of getting hurt again. I've been through a lot with Eric, and I thought coming here would be a way to move on, but I didn't expect to meet someone like you. And it's throwing me off balance. I don't know how to deal with it."

Jake's brow furrowed, and he took a step closer, his voice gentle. "You think I'm not scared? I've been keeping people at arm's length for years because of what happened with my family, but...this weekend, with you, it's been different. You're different."

Phoebe looked up at him, her heart pounding as his words

sank in. "I thought you were pulling away because you didn't care."

Jake shook his head. "I wasn't pulling away because I didn't care. I was pulling away because I *do* care. Too much, maybe. And I wasn't sure you wanted the same thing."

They stood there in the quiet warmth of the beach, the sound of the ocean filling the space between them. For the first time, Phoebe could see the vulnerability in Jake's eyes, the guardedness he'd been hiding behind his sarcasm and cynicism. And she realized that maybe they weren't so different after all—both of them afraid to let someone in, both of them trying to protect themselves from the possibility of getting hurt again.

"I'm sorry," Phoebe whispered, taking a step closer, her voice soft but sure. "I don't want to run away from this. I'm scared, but I don't want to lose whatever this is."

Jake reached out, gently brushing a strand of hair behind her ear, his touch sending a shiver down her spine. "You're not going to lose it, Phoebe. I'm not going anywhere. But I need you to be honest with me. Can you do that?"

Phoebe nodded, her heart racing as she looked up at him. "Yeah. I can."

For a moment, neither of them moved, the air between them charged with something unspoken. Then, as if some invisible barrier had finally crumbled, Jake leaned in, pressing his lips to hers in a kiss that was slow, deep, and filled with all the words they hadn't yet said.

When they finally pulled apart, both of them breathless, Phoebe smiled, her heart lighter than it had been in months.

"Christmas Eve at 80 degrees," she said with a laugh, glancing around at the surreal tropical holiday setting. "Who would've thought?"

Jake grinned, his hand still resting on her cheek. "Hey, if it brings us here, I'm not complaining."

They stood there for a while longer, the bonfire crackling in the distance, the sounds of laughter and music floating on the breeze. But here, in the quiet glow of the tiki torches, it felt like the heart of the storm had finally passed.

And in its place, something new—something real—was beginning.

Mistletoe & Mimosas

The next morning, the sun was already high in the sky, casting a golden glow over Noel Beach Resort's pool area. The "Mistletoe & Mimosas" brunch was in full swing, with guests milling about in festive swimwear, sipping mimosas, and laughing under the fluttering mistletoe strategically hung over every table and lounge chair.

Phoebe sat by the pool, her feet dangling in the cool water as she sipped her own mimosa, feeling far more at ease than she had in days. The tension between her and Jake had dissolved after last night's conversation, and now, there was an easy warmth between them, as if the emotional storm they'd weathered had cleared the air for something deeper.

Jake appeared at her side, holding two fresh mimosas and giving her a playful smirk as he handed her one. "You look way too comfortable. Ready for round two?"

Phoebe smiled, accepting the drink. "I think I've earned it after all the holiday chaos."

He sat down next to her, letting his legs stretch out beside hers in the water. The morning air was warm but breezy, and the sound of laughter and clinking glasses filled the air, creating a light, festive atmosphere that no longer felt overwhelming. Maybe it was because she wasn't fighting it anymore. Or maybe it was because of Jake.

"You've come a long way from grumbling about candy canes," Jake teased, raising his glass to her.

Phoebe rolled her eyes but clinked her glass with his. "Don't get too smug. I'm still not a Christmas fanatic, but I'll admit, I'm enjoying myself a little more than I expected."

Jake grinned, his eyes twinkling. "Is it the mimosas or the mistletoe?"

Phoebe glanced up at the little sprig of mistletoe dangling from an umbrella above them and laughed. "Oh, definitely the mistletoe. It's magical, haven't you heard?"

Jake leaned in slightly, his voice low and teasing. "Maybe we should test that theory."

Phoebe's heart fluttered as he closed the distance between them, brushing his lips lightly against hers in a soft, lingering kiss. It was sweet and playful, a perfect reflection of the easy, joyful mood of the morning. When they pulled apart, she felt warmth spread through her, both from the kiss and the realization that something had shifted between them—something that felt more solid, more real than before.

"Yep," Jake said, pulling back with a grin, "definitely the mistletoe."

They shared a laugh, the tension from the previous days melting away entirely. For the first time, Phoebe felt like she wasn't carrying the weight of her past or her fears about the future. Right here, right now, it was just her and Jake, and the world felt lighter.

As they sipped their drinks and soaked up the sun, Jake shifted a little, his expression softening. "Hey, I was thinking," he began, his tone a little more serious, "if you're not too busy later, maybe you'd want to check out the marine biology center. I could show you some of the work I've been doing with the sharks."

Phoebe raised an eyebrow, pleasantly surprised by the invitation. "Really? You want to show me?"

Jake nodded, his gaze steady. "Yeah. I know it's not exactly festive, but it's a big part of my life. And...I don't usually share that with people."

The quiet sincerity in his voice made Phoebe's heart skip a beat. This wasn't just a casual invite. This was Jake letting her in, showing her a part of himself he didn't easily reveal to others. She smiled, touched by the gesture.

"I'd love to see it," she said, her voice soft.

Jake's expression relaxed, and he looked genuinely pleased. "Great. I'll show you what I've been working on after the storm disrupted our fieldwork. I think you'll like it."

LATER THAT AFTERNOON, after a morning of mimosas and lighthearted fun by the pool, Jake drove Phoebe a short distance to the marine biology center where he worked. The building was small and understated, nestled near the shoreline, with windows that looked out onto the sparkling blue ocean. Inside, the air was cool and quiet, a peaceful contrast to the bustling resort.

As Jake led her through the halls, explaining the various research projects, Phoebe felt a sense of calm wash over her. This was Jake's world—a world of careful study, of protecting and understanding marine life. And as he talked about his work with a quiet passion, she realized how much of himself he poured into it, even though he downplayed it with his usual casual demeanor.

"So, this is the part where the magic happens," Jake said, leading her into a large room filled with tanks and monitoring equipment. Several of the tanks housed small sharks, their sleek bodies gliding gracefully through the water as they circled their enclosures.

Phoebe watched in awe, fascinated by the creatures. "Wow. They're beautiful."

Jake smiled, his eyes lighting up as he leaned on the edge of one of the tanks. "Yeah, they are. This is one of the projects we've been working on—tracking how environmental changes are affecting their migration patterns. It's...important work, but not always glamorous."

Phoebe shook her head. "Are you kidding? This is amazing. You're actually making a difference."

Jake shrugged, but there was a glint of pride in his eyes. "I guess. It feels good to do something that matters."

Phoebe glanced at him, feeling a surge of admiration. "You really love it, don't you? Even if it's not always easy."

Jake nodded, his expression softening. "Yeah. I've always been more comfortable with sharks than people, I guess. They don't expect anything from you, they just are. But lately..." He trailed off, meeting her gaze. "You've kind of thrown me off my game."

Phoebe smiled, her heart swelling at his honesty. "In a good way, I hope."

Jake chuckled, his hand brushing lightly against hers. "Yeah, in a good way."

They stood there in comfortable silence, the gentle hum of the tanks around them, and for the first time since they met, Phoebe felt like she was seeing the real Jake—the man who cared deeply, who worked tirelessly for something bigger than himself, even if he didn't always show it. And she realized that what had started as a simple distraction, as two people bonding over their shared dislike of holiday chaos, had turned into something much deeper.

"You know," Jake said after a moment, his voice quiet but warm, "I'm glad you ended up at the resort. Even if it was because you were dragged there."

Phoebe laughed softly. "Me too. I wasn't expecting any of this, but I'm glad it happened."

Jake squeezed her hand gently, his eyes holding hers. "So...what happens after Christmas?"

Phoebe hesitated for a split second, feeling the weight of that question, but then smiled. "I guess we'll have to figure that out. But I'd like to see where this goes. You and me, beyond the holiday chaos."

Jake smiled, his expression soft and sincere. "Me too."

As they stood there together, surrounded by the quiet hum of Jake's world, Phoebe realized that what they'd found wasn't just a fleeting holiday fling. It was something real, something worth holding onto.

And for the first time in a long time, she wasn't scared to see where it might lead.

Love in the Keys

The sun hung low in the sky, casting a golden-orange glow over Noel Beach Resort as the holiday weekend began to wind down. The palm trees swayed gently in the breeze, and the festive decorations that had seemed so absurd to Phoebe just days ago now felt like part of a magical backdrop. The resort was still buzzing with guests enjoying their last taste of the Christmas-in-July celebration, but for Phoebe, everything had taken on a quieter, more reflective tone.

She stood on the balcony of her bungalow, watching the waves roll lazily onto the shore, her mind swirling with thoughts about what came next. Her suitcase was half-packed, her flight back to New York scheduled for the next morning, but the thought of leaving the Florida Keys, of leaving *Jake*, tugged at her heart.

It had all happened so fast. What had started as an escape from her messy breakup had turned into something so much more. Jake had broken down her defenses, shown her a side of himself that he didn't easily share with others, and in doing so, had helped her see a future she hadn't dared to imagine.

The sound of footsteps approaching pulled her from her

thoughts. She turned to see Jake walking up the path to her bungalow, a quiet smile on his face. He wore his usual board shorts and faded T-shirt, his hair tousled from the wind, and even though he looked as casual as ever, there was something different in his eyes—something softer, more vulnerable.

"Hey," he said, stopping at the foot of the stairs.

"Hey," Phoebe replied, her heart doing that familiar flutter in her chest.

Jake glanced up at her, then nodded toward the beach. "I was thinking...we should take a walk. One last night under the stars before the holiday madness ends."

Phoebe smiled, feeling a rush of warmth at the idea. "I'd like that."

She grabbed a light sweater and joined him as they made their way down to the beach. The sand was cool beneath their feet, the sky painted in shades of pink and purple as the sun dipped closer to the horizon. Twinkling Christmas lights strung along the resort's palm trees reflected off the water, giving the entire scene a surreal but beautiful glow.

For a while, they walked in comfortable silence, the waves lapping gently at their ankles, neither of them wanting to break the peace of the moment. But as the soft light of the setting sun faded into twilight, Phoebe knew they couldn't avoid the inevitable conversation any longer.

"What happens next?" she asked quietly, her voice barely above a whisper.

Jake stopped, turning to face her. He looked out at the horizon for a moment, as if gathering his thoughts, before meeting her gaze. "That's the question, isn't it?"

Phoebe nodded, her chest tightening as the weight of the situation settled in. "I'm supposed to go back to New York tomorrow."

"And I'm supposed to stay here," Jake said, his tone tinged with uncertainty. "I've got my work, my life here. But..."

He trailed off, and Phoebe held her breath, waiting for him to continue.

"But the last few days with you have made me realize that maybe there's more to life than what I've been holding onto. I've spent so long keeping people at a distance, not wanting to get hurt, but with you...it's different."

Phoebe felt her heart swell at his words. "It's different for me, too," she admitted. "I didn't expect this. I came here to get away from everything, and instead, I found...you."

Jake smiled, taking a step closer. "So, what do we do about it?"

Phoebe let out a soft laugh, her emotions swirling. "I don't know. I wasn't expecting to have this kind of connection with someone, let alone while surrounded by inflatable snowmen and jet-skiing Santas."

Jake chuckled, the sound deep and warm, before his expression turned more serious. "I don't want this to end, Phoebe. But I also don't want to pressure you into making a decision."

Phoebe appreciated his honesty, but the thought of leaving him—of walking away from what they'd found—made her chest tighten with a sense of loss she wasn't ready to face.

"I don't want it to end either," she said softly. "But my life is in New York. My job, my apartment...everything."

Jake nodded, understanding in his eyes. "I get that. And I'm not asking you to give all that up. But maybe you don't have to make a decision right now. Maybe you could stay a little longer—see where this goes. No pressure, no big decisions. Just...us."

Phoebe looked up at him, her heart racing as she considered his words. The old her—the one who guarded herself fiercely and didn't take risks—would have balked at the idea of staying longer, of pushing back her return to her orderly, predictable life in New York. But the new her, the one Jake had brought to the surface, was willing to take a chance.

"I could do that," she said, a slow smile spreading across her face. "I could stay a little longer."

Jake's face lit up with relief and something deeper—hope. "Yeah?"

"Yeah," Phoebe replied, feeling a weight lift from her shoulders. "Let's see where this goes."

Jake reached out, pulling her gently into his arms. As they stood there, the waves lapping at their feet and the twinkling lights of the resort casting a soft glow around them, Phoebe felt something settle inside her—a quiet certainty that whatever came next, they would face it together.

"I'm glad you're staying," Jake whispered, his lips brushing her forehead.

Phoebe looked up at him, her eyes filled with warmth. "So am I."

They stood there for a long moment, the ocean stretching out before them, the stars beginning to twinkle in the darkening sky. And as the sounds of the resort's final holiday festivities carried through the air, Phoebe realized that for the first time in a long while, she wasn't worried about what the future held.

Because in this moment, with Jake by her side, it felt like everything had fallen into place.

And whatever happened next—whether it was in the Florida Keys or somewhere else—they would figure it out, together.

Epilogue: Christmas in July... Again?

Six months later, the Florida sun was just as warm and welcoming as Phoebe remembered, but this time, everything felt different. This time, there was no reluctance, no hesitation. As she stepped off the shuttle bus and onto the sandy path leading to Noel Beach Resort, a smile tugged at her lips.

Phoebe glanced up at the familiar "Welcome to Noel Beach Resort!" sign, still decked out in twinkling lights and garland, with oversized candy canes planted next to the palm trees. Instead of rolling her eyes at the holiday chaos, she found herself grinning at the sight of it.

Christmas in July. Who would have thought she'd be excited to be back for this ridiculous tradition?

Jake stood beside her, carrying their bags with a relaxed ease. He caught her smile and raised an eyebrow, a teasing glint in his ocean-blue eyes. "I remember a time when you thought this place was your worst nightmare."

Phoebe laughed, reaching for his hand. "Yeah, well, things change."

"Do they?" he teased, tugging her playfully toward him.

Epilogue: Christmas in July... Again?

"Because last I checked, there's still an inflatable snowman melting in the sun over there."

Phoebe glanced over at the slightly deflated snowman, which was leaning precariously to one side, and couldn't help but laugh. "Okay, maybe not everything has changed."

Jake grinned, squeezing her hand. "But you have."

Phoebe smiled at that, knowing he was right. A lot had changed in the past six months—most of all, her. When she'd first arrived at Noel Beach Resort, she had been lost, recovering from heartbreak, and trying to escape her life. Now, she had found something she hadn't expected: love, with Jake, and a new way of seeing the world.

They were back at the resort not just for another "Christmas in July" celebration, but for the fun of it. And this time, they were ready to embrace all of its quirks—together.

"Come on, we've got a title to defend," Jake said, nudging her with his elbow.

"Oh, right," Phoebe replied, her excitement bubbling up as they made their way toward the beach. "The reigning sandman-building champions can't disappoint."

They reached the competition area where groups of families and couples were already busy shaping their sandy creations. This year, Phoebe was all in. The beach was packed with festive energy—seashell ornaments, tinsel draped over surfboards, and people in Santa hats sculpting their sandmen with intense concentration.

Phoebe and Jake found their spot, setting down their bags and grabbing their tools. They'd spent weeks joking about how to outdo last year's creation, and now, the playful competition between them was back in full swing.

"Alright, champion," Phoebe said with mock seriousness, shoveling sand into a pile. "What's the strategy?"

Jake rubbed his chin as if deep in thought. "I'm thinking we go

Epilogue: Christmas in July... Again?

big this time. Triple-tier sandman, seashell buttons, maybe a mini snowdog to top it off."

Phoebe giggled, loving how easily they fell into this rhythm together. "I like it. But we're definitely adding a sand Santa hat this year."

They spent the next hour building their masterpiece, their hands covered in sand and their faces flushed from the sun. It was easy, carefree—everything their first trip hadn't been, but everything this new chapter in their lives was. They laughed at each other's attempts to perfect the sandman's nose, bickered good-naturedly over the design, and, in the end, created something that was far from perfect but utterly theirs.

As the contest wrapped up, they stood back to admire their creation—taller than last year's, with a seashell-studded scarf and a sand Santa hat perched crookedly on its head. It wasn't about winning, though Phoebe had to admit she wouldn't mind holding onto the champion title. It was about the fun they'd had together.

When the final judgment came, they didn't win first place—but they didn't care. They'd won something better.

Later that evening, after the chaos of the contest had settled and the resort was lit up for another tropical holiday night, Phoebe and Jake found themselves back on the beach, this time with mimosas in hand. The sun was just beginning to set, casting a soft, golden light over the water, and the Christmas lights twinkled in the palm trees behind them.

They sat down on the sand, leaning back against each other, their legs stretched out in front of them as they watched the horizon.

"You know," Phoebe said, her voice soft, "last year, I couldn't wait to get away from here."

Jake chuckled, his arm wrapping around her shoulders. "And now?"

She smiled, leaning her head against his chest. "Now, I kind of love it. The madness, the weird holiday traditions, even the sand snowmen. It's all...good. Because it's us."

Jake kissed the top of her head, his voice low and warm. "It's definitely us."

They watched the sun dip below the horizon, the sky turning a deep shade of purple, and Phoebe felt the familiar sense of peace wash over her. This was her life now—a life she hadn't planned for but one she was more than ready to embrace.

"I'm glad I stayed a little longer," Phoebe said quietly, her fingers intertwining with Jake's.

Jake smiled, his eyes soft as he looked down at her. "Me too."

They sat there in comfortable silence, the sound of the waves and the distant hum of the resort behind them, knowing that whatever came next, they would face it together. And as the last light of the day faded, Phoebe felt a quiet certainty settle in her heart.

This was just the beginning.

And whatever the future held—Christmas in July or otherwise—they were ready for it.

Afterword from the Author: Bree Winterson

When I first sat down to write *Christmas in July*, I knew I wanted to create a holiday romance that was a little different from the ones we're used to seeing. I've always loved the magic of Christmas—twinkling lights, the smell of pine trees, the cozy winter scenes we often associate with the season—but I wondered, *what if we could capture that same magic in a completely unexpected setting?* What if, instead of snow and hot cocoa, we had palm trees, sandcastles, and surfboards? What if we took the spirit of the holidays and dropped it right into the middle of a tropical paradise?

And that's where the idea for Noel Beach Resort was born.

I wanted to explore the idea that holiday traditions don't have to follow the same formula. Whether it's Christmas in July, jet-skiing Santas, or building a sandman under a blazing sun, the holiday spirit can show up in all kinds of unexpected ways. In Phoebe and Jake's story, I saw a chance to explore how love and connection can surprise us, even when we're not looking for it—especially when we're not looking for it. Their romance unfolds in a place that's far from the snowy winter wonderland we usually

Afterword from the Author: Bree Winterson

imagine, but the magic of the holidays is still there, shining through in the most unlikely moments.

For me, this story is a reminder that love often finds us when we least expect it—and that sometimes, stepping out of our comfort zones leads to the greatest adventures. Phoebe came to Noel Beach to escape, and Jake had long since closed himself off from letting anyone get too close, but together, they discovered that the things we think we're running from can be the very things that open us up to new possibilities.

As I wrote about the quirky holiday traditions, from the sand-man-building contest to the mistletoe moments and tropical Christmas cocktails, I wanted to capture the joy of letting go, of finding fun in the chaos, and of embracing the beauty of being a little unconventional. The story of Phoebe and Jake is proof that there's magic in breaking away from the expected—whether it's in love, in life, or in the way we celebrate the holidays.

So, to all my readers, I encourage you to find your own "Christmas in July" moments—those times when life takes you somewhere you didn't plan on going, but it turns out to be exactly where you needed to be. Embrace the unexpected, dive into new experiences, and don't be afraid to create your own traditions along the way. Because, as Phoebe and Jake learned, sometimes the most magical moments happen when we're open to celebrating the unexpected.

Thank you for joining me on this tropical holiday adventure. I hope this story brought a little warmth and joy to your heart, no matter the season.

With love and sunshine, **Bree Winterson**

www.ingramcontent.com/pod-product-compliance
Lightning Source LLC
LaVergne TN
LVHW051058100526
838202LV00086BA/6937